Jeff and the Fiery Forge

Jeff and the Fiery Forge

Nathan Ogbechie

Published by

Pan-Atlantic University Press
KM 52 Lekki-Epe Express Road
Ibeju-Lekki, Lagos State, Nigeria
paupress.pau.edu.ng paupress@pau.edu.ng

A catalogue record of this book is available on request from the National Library of Nigeria.

ISBN: 978-978-60817-5-5

Contents

AUTHOR'S NOTE

This book was inspired by my love for *Minecraft*, a sandbox game originally released in 2009. It was created using the Java programming language. In the game, players explore a blocky, pixelated, procedurally generated, three-dimensional world with virtually infinite terrain. Players can discover and extract raw materials, craft tools and items, and build structures, earthworks, and machines. The wide range of possibilities in *Minecraft* expanded my imagination and enabled me to write a book that pushes the boundaries of creativity and challenges conventional thinking.

Jeff and the Fiery Forge is about a teenage boy who goes on an amazing adventure in a world threatened by a vicious tribe called the redminers. The reader will follow Jeff's journey as he makes new friends, reunites with old friends and navigates through the various obstacles that come his way.

I would like to thank my family for allowing me to express myself with this book and giving me pointers that ensure readers get maximum satisfaction. Special mention to my dad – Alex Ogbechie, Mum – Nkem Ogbechie, sister – Nia-Marie Ogbechie, grandpa – Sir Professor Chris Ogbechie and aunt – Thelma Obiakor, for the countless hours spent editing the book for me.

I would also like to thank my two grandmas, my other grandpa, uncles and aunties who continuously motivated me to keep writing. Uncle Emeka Ogbechie, Uncle Nnamdi Ogbechie, Aunt Ij

Ogbechie, Aunt Ekene Ogbechie, Aunt Aisha Ogbechie, Aunt Rosario Ogbechie, Aunt Amina Asalu, Aunt Abi Maduakor and Aunt Nkiru Osoba. I hope you all enjoy the book.

PROLOGUE

"We need to imprison him!" said a soldier from the tribe of the royal redminers.

"Yes...maybe in our metal cage with the dreadful silverbugs that scavenge our place," another soldier added.

"He has come too far into our habitat!" said another soldier, apprehensively.

Jeff, an adventurous 14-year-old with fluffy brown hair, recognised for his rumpled red hoodie, rusty old boots and backpack, has scavenged the world of legends. The same world is intruded on by the vicious royal redminers.

Jeff lives in a wooden hut. He uses two big boxes to store artefacts, a table to forge, a magical table to enchant things and a table for crafting. He also has a few chests and a jukebox to listen to music. He has a few pictures of his family who died in a car crash, trophies of some of his greatest achievements, and finally, equipment for adventures.

Chapter 1

THE FLAMING PLAN

On an average summer night with a calm breeze and peaceful atmosphere, Jeff thought it would be a good idea to go on another adventure. Gazing at the bright stars, which reminded him of the time he fought a superhuman verdeling, Jeff felt the urge to fight again. "The world is so infamous! I wonder what other things are out there," he thought.

"Well, I better get to work," Jeff muttered to himself, getting charmed by the beauty of the night. Before he could get up, he heard the noise of digging and groaning. It was a verdeling.

"Oh no, not those again!" he exclaimed. Verdeling zombies were rising from the dead, along with skeletons and rascals of the mines.

The verdelings are skinny, human-like creatures, covered with black and green spots. They have very long arms–so long that they drag on the surface with dust trailing behind, and green orbs that cut through their torsos.

The rascals are dwarfs with hunchbacks and immense speed. They also carry mystery boxes. "Hehehe," a rascal cackled. Jeff ran, grabbing his map from his backpack. He was looking through the map while trying to escape the beasts chasing behind him. A verdeling almost got him but he was able to turn in another direction just in time. He was frightened.

Deep in the redshift mines, the royal redminers gathered up in one space:

"...and you will come up with a plan to end that puny boy once and for all," ordered the king of the redminers, Roland Maverick. "Yes, master!" the soldiers replied "How he has managed to outwit most of you filthy, annoying peasants is beyond me!" the king added. Roland was small for a king; in fact, he was as small as the average dustbin. He had a big nose (like a blobfish), grey skin and a golden crown.

The redminers got to work on an awesome robot made with iron, blackstone, redstone, heated rocks, solar rocks and pistons. The redcraft figure was ready. "Yes! My creation-" the king got cut off, "Our creation is complete," said a redminer chief. "Did you just cut me off?" asked the king. "Now, you have to be punished."

The king ordered the redcraft figure to destroy him. "No, please, I didn't mean to! I'm sorry. Please don't hurt me! I will do anything, I promise!" cried the chief. "You promise? Well, I order you to shut up and stand in front of the redcraft figure!" yelled the king. The chief did so in fear and trepidation. The chief screamed as the figure stretched its piston hand to crush him. "Do you have any last words?" the figure asked, with its robotic voice. "Give this to my family," the chief replied; he gave the redcraft figure a piece of paper which read: I love you with all my might, never forget me. The redcraft figure handed the paper to the king, and he ripped it into tiny pieces.

The redcraft figure devoured its prey vigorously.

"That was delightful!" said the redcraft, joyfully.

"Does anyone else want to volunteer?" yelled the king.

"No, sire!" replied all the redminers. A day later, five of the redminers were pondering along with a geominer. Geominers were people who had special tools to mine big places; they had a purple glowing strap around their neck, a brown chestplate, and a giant wrench with a purple glow.

"So, first I need to find his location-" the geominer got cut off, "How? Maybe clues?" said a redminer.

"For dust's sake, YES," said the geominer with a scowl.

***

Jeff was strolling through fields of great green grass as the sun was rising.

"Ahh, I love the mornings!" Jeff breathed in happiness. He looked up and spotted a tower with a few redwatchers (redminers that stay on the lookout), and a redwood lumberjack chopping wood near the tower.

"Keep an eye out for intruders, especially that goofy boy," the lumberjack said with an Australian accent.

"I know, right," replied a redwatcher. "So, what did that boy even do to that maniac of a king? I only got hired recently."

"Apparently, the king and Jeff have a *history* that I know nothing about," the lumberjack said.

Jeff frowned and rolled his eyes, "Great! This will be fun!"

He stopped for a water break and then brought out his sword along with his special brew, the shadow brew. He drank it and snuck into the tower. "It sure is beautiful out there," said a redwatcher. "Yeah, but who is that? He drank the forbidden potion, the shadow brew!" another redwatcher said, panicking. This made the redwatchers take the job more seriously. "Oh my! This place has quite a lot of good loot! I found a glaive; they will be jealous." whispered Jeff joyfully. "When I get back, I can enchant it! Yep, I will." Jeff revealed himself and the redwatchers started screaming.

"HAHAHA!" cackled Jeff just as he disabled his shadow brew. He struck hard at a redwatcher. The redwatcher groaned angrily, "Intruder!" Jeff sliced and diced all the redwatchers with his shiny glaive, but then the redwood lumberjack came charging at him with his glowing red metal axe. Jeff dodged it with a side flip and pierced his glaive right through his metal chestplate. "I think he's tired," said Jeff. "Welp, I better get to the mountain. This glaive is good," said Jeff happily. Jeff left the tower, knowing more challenges lay ahead. He ran through fields and took frequent water breaks. "Holy cow! Do I see a big chunky pig?!" shouted Jeff. He went and sliced the pig into pieces and kept it. "I'm gonna have to fry these!" Jeff ran and ran, but then he tripped on a rock and face-planted on the grass. "Ouch, I think I should slow down," he said.

"AAAAARGH! That's it! I thought you slaves were useful but you keep getting killed by that thirteen-year-old boy... I mean fourteen. Think of a plan and I want to see everyone at the deepest depths of the redmines [also known as the deep redmines!]" raged the king. "Yes sir!" replied the redminers. The next day, they got to the deep redmines. "So, we have different parts of this civilization, right?" said the king. Everyone nodded.

"We are having different bases, and when I say bases, I mean places near the terrible terra, and it is not terrible, it is just dangerous; it is going to be called the highblock hallways. It will include most of you redminers, redwatchers, red-archers, redmedics, red-deads, red-wilds, evokers, redwood lumberjacks, illusionists, hermes, guards, redhikers, geominers, chiefs, brutes, horsemen, red-lanterns, ruinous damage (ravager), hazmats and finally the second and third superior commanders and demanders." ordered the king. "Yes sir," everyone else said. "And not all of you can be there, only two of each," the king said calmly. He ordered a bulky brute to throw him to his glazed red crystal throne.

A red-lantern walked out into the morning with a lantern in his hand, but his red, feathered bird started chirping [each red-lantern has a red bird to tell others who is boss and summon evil life] "Ok," said a red-lantern. "They should get to work because I don't want to see something terrible." thought the king. "Speak up please!" yelled a red-wild (red-wilds and red-deads can read minds and they are known as the BEST fakers). "Don't worry!" the king shouted back.

Jeff stopped at a tree and held his map in front of him. He pondered where to go; "The redmines would be cool; maybe the snowy summits?" Then he brought out the blueprint of a base he wanted to build; it was made out of mangrove wood and a bit of crimson powder *(it helps things sprout, creating beautiful sceneries).* The base would be in a cylinder shape with little bumps on the bottom. Jeff imagined that the base would look very good. He spent a few nights and days building, spending, and asking. "Finally," sighed Jeff, "It's complete!" Jeff went inside. It was bigger than he thought. He just had to move everything from his former house to this new one, but as he did, a red storm raged and he started feeling like his lungs were weakening. He couldn't breathe properly.

The high block halls were almost finished. It was a great masterpiece, made out of black minerals, and shiny as an amethyst gemstone. "That is so cool." Jeff coughed as he tried to move his stuff as fast as he could. Surprisingly, he was fast enough, but the feeling in his lungs was getting worse. He needed to drink a special potion—the potion of resistance, but they were only at the royal ruins. The royal ruins was the former castle of the king of the redminers. A man named Martin Davidson made a hybrid called the spectre; it hunts people who haven't regained any energy for more than 3 days. It looks like a bat, but it is covered in a dark blue, webbed coating and has large, menacing, yellow eyes. The spectre destroyed the castle so the king had to move away, however, he left valuables such as the potion of resistance. Jeff put a pin on the royal ruins and then wrapped his toilet paper around it. He set off, feeling the striking pain in his lungs and knowing that something far worse would soon come.

"Ow!" Jeff exclaimed as he stepped on a piece of sharp redstone; it was a piece from the ancient redcraft chassis. It was like the redcraft figure but it was rustier; it had solar rocks as its eyes, and had a giant rusted piece of redstone on its back as its core. It also had redstone horns and a big lower jaw. Jeff glanced at the piece and an interesting thought crossed his mind. He decided to make his own golem! He needed more parts though, and he couldn't forget about the blazing resistance potion. "Jeez! I should have gotten something to speed this up," said Jeff, but then he saw rusty old swiftness boots. [These were boots that increased your speed when running or sprinting.] The boots were lying on the green grass. "Yes!! Swiftness boots!" celebrated

Jeff as he put them on. He got faster and used less energy. Then, he got to the woods, a decaying forest.

Chapter 2

THE WITHERING WOODS

The woods were getting withered. The grass was dark and silverbugs were scavenging the place. The trees had jittering ghostly wisps muffled in the dead leaves. Jeff saw something he wasn't expecting to see—a dead cornflower with pink particles sprouting around it. "That's weird. Has a flower done all this damage?" he thought to himself. He then pulled it out and realised that the soil had blue sparks springing out of it and this caused the damage in the forest.

"Thanks, we've been trapped in this beast!" said a spark.

"Yeah, I would give you a gift if I could!" said another.

"Star!" a third spark said.

Jeff noticed that the soil started changing into a weird shape. As this was happening, a skull emerged, and then two others, alongside a dark ribcage. The ribcage shot out a black mist; the decaying skull-fly had awakened. It rose and roared ferociously, and shot its skulls at the trees and surrounding animals. It then tried going for Jeff. "Sorry mister, but that's not gonna work!" yelled the boy as he blocked the skull with his glaive. Jeff got into a ninja pose and dashed at the skull-fly, slicing it many times. The skull-fly roared as it went to its next phase; lightning-blue aura was blazing around it and it spawned skeletons.

Jeff wasn't taking any chances. He quickly got a book out of his bag—the updraft book [it sent chosen monsters into the air and smashed them back down]. Jeff used it to smash the skeletons into pieces. He finally got close to the skull-fly and attempted his strongest slash ever. The glaive turned purple and SLASH! The skull-fly was defeated. "You are a true hero," said a blue spark. Just when Jeff was about to relax, a silverbug pounced onto his face. "Get it off!" Jeff panicked as he was trying to pull the bug off *(silverbugs can poison others when they are on a host for too long)*. A minute passed and Jeff was finally able to pull the bug off. He looked at the corpse of the decaying skull-fly knowing there was more to come.

Jeff ran through the woods endlessly. He noticed a haunter following him. Jeff tried his best to ignore it but it kept catching his eye and making spooky noises; it seemed it wanted his attention. "Whoever you are, show yourself," Jeff called out as he had gotten too uncomfortable. Jeff held his glaive in horror, glancing at his surroundings as something started taking over his mind.

(Haunters are dwarf-sized humanoid creatures without a lower half. They are ghosts who burn places with blue fire and take over minds., They have physical skull faces and can go invisible anytime they want. Ghostbusters are capable of catching them.)

Finally, Jeff touched the haunter's face, and the haunter became visible. It made weird noises and flew away, slowly. "That was spooky!" said Jeff. He carried on with his adventure. While strolling through the woods, he saw an ancient hut. "Hello? Is anyone here?" called Jeff; but no one was there except a few brewing stands, a cauldron, and a lost kitty. The kitty meowed in pain. "Oh no, what's wrong, kitty?" Jeff asked whilst scratching its neck, but the kitty hissed and scratched him back. The kitty had quite a lot of fleas and was pretty young.

Jeff looked left and right, wondering if anyone was watching, then he carried the kitty and put it in his backpack (his bag is of high technology so it has the capacity to store even a kitty). Jeff cancelled his mission for the day because the sun was setting and he had to get home to aid the lost kitty. The kitty meowed several times. "Don't worry, it's okay little buddy, we will be home soon," said Jeff as he comforted the kitty. The kitty turned out to be female. Jeff finally got home; by then all sunlight had disappeared. He put a collar on her neck and named her Joy. He wanted her name to start with a "J". He took out her fleas and gave her a treat; she was now loving and energised. Jeff placed the kitty next to his bed and went to sleep. "Nighty!" Jeff whispered as he covered himself. The plan was ready.

Joy meowed and tapped Jeff's face. He was asleep, so now she could go hunting. She scratched the window and made a crack in it, one that was big enough for her to pass. She strolled past zombies, rascals, rats, and silverbugs. She looked up at the stars but didn't find them promising; it looked like they were telling her, "He doesn't love you, he just wants a slave. Don't judge the human by his cover, Feel free." Jeff loved Joy, and she believed it too. She thought back to the stars, "He really does love me. He really does. It's been an hour but we already have chemistry! I can feel it. I have seen his eyes and I believe we are really partners in friendship! Rats and cats fight, but it is like we are cat and cat. We bond together!" a tear trickled down Joy's cheek, and she had the cutest face ever as she reassured herself of her friendship with Jeff, and then game face was on.

Joy was starting to have the instinct of a true predator. She sprinted swiftly, jumped three feet into the air, caught a small spectre and took its corpse. *(Spectres are like owls but have small green eyes and navy-blue reptile skin).* Joy then went to the closest stream and caught five fishes. She was satisfied and ready to return home; the time was 4:00 am. Joy meowed and touched Jeff's forehead, calmly checking if he was awake. She put her loot beside him cautiously and fell asleep on top of him.

Moments later, Jeff woke up to see the kitty on his lap, fast asleep. He also saw the loot she brought. He picked up a fish and glanced at it, seeing the bite marks. The fish blinked and wriggled, so Jeff squeezed it tight so it stopped breathing. Jeff got out of bed, went to his furnace, and cooked the fish. It was now a fine, oily, salty fish, ready to be eaten. Jeff took a large bite, and it was a delightful sensation.

He had the rest and changed into his adventure clothes. Joy woke up and yawned. Jeff put her in his backpack and set off. He ran with his blue swiftness boots and he noticed a portal with a shiny metamorphic rock, and another portal, this one purple with endless black. "Uuuuuh, I'm not gonna go in, no way, only stupid people will do-" he got cut off as he was sucked in; it was like a black hole. "WHOOOAAAAA!!!!!!" Jeff shouted as he swirled and twisted in the portal until he got out on the other side. It was dark, the floor was red and there was no water - it was lava.

There were burning blue flames and skulls everywhere. Jeff looked on and saw the same souls from the woods and the same soil he had encountered there, only this time, the soil was split in two parts. Soul soil and soul sand. Soul soil had many holes in it, while soul sand was very dense and had tiny souls living in it. Due to its density, Jeff could move faster on it but he had to be careful as it produced something even stronger than the decaying skull-fly. Jeff got out a book named *The*

Enchanting Spells. "Hmm, this will be complicated," said Jeff as he opened the book. He saw forbidden writings of the howling voids. "Uhhhh, guess I'll just say some gibberish and hope I get a good enchantment!" thought Jeff. He then said something close to, "May I have a powerful upgrade?"

The book and his glaive started to float, and letters started spilling out of the book. The glaive's colour changed to tinted purple, and it dropped to his hand, with a new name: *sharpness spell*. So, I got sharpness?" He thought. He then touched the tip with his finger which made a small mark appear. He licked his finger and carried the glaive carefully. Jeff walked, looking both ways in panic, and then he saw something in the air that looked like a large white jellyfish with a small but menacing face; it roared and shot a fireball at him. Jeff spotted the fireball and was able to evade it. He dodged four of these fireballs as he pondered to himself, "I can't keep on dodging these. What happens if I hit it back with my glaive?"

He looked behind him and saw the burning flames and craters that the jellyfish created. Jeff started to call the ugly cloud-looking thing a ghost. A fireball was coming his way, but this time, he hit it back hard with his glaive and it smashed the ghost in the face. It fell to the ground and rolled off a rocky red cliff. Jeff was shocked as the ghost-looking monster splashed and formed a pattern of bubbling lava. "Yes, the ghost is gone!" Jeff celebrated with a small dance, then he continued his journey through the dimension (it is called the wretched dimension).

He walked and walked until he got to a point where the bumpy red rock had now become a hard type of grey rock. Magma jellies sploshed and squelched noisily as they roamed the everlasting lava oceans; crimson and teal forests of subterrestrial nature crowded the place. Jeff looked in the forest and saw a small village which was surprisingly calm. He saw a molten golem whacking a fiery superhuman into the trees, villagers selling items to each other, silverbugs crawling around the village, and stone servers (they are small golems who follow people around and obey their commands).

"Oh my gally geese, this place is huge," said Jeff in astonishment as a villager came up to him.

"O fellow traveller, welcome to aye ugly wretched dimension!" Then a farmer came up to Jeff. "We have lots of food, but git away from aye molten golem, he can crush ya to tiny pieces!"

Jeff spent a day there and he slept well, although on the floor. After his slumber, he woke up to see the village in flames. He couldn't believe his eyes. While processing everything, he saw a child running up to him crying, "Help! The redminers are attacking the village!"

It turned out the redminers tracked his portal. Jeff pondered a bit and realised what he must do. He said to himself, "*Explore and seek, find the needs, be brave and come in peace.*" He said this to himself multiple times and then fled from the tiny town. As he fled, something came in his way; it was a little golem called a ministrosity. It was tiny and had tiny arms, black patches around its body and a glowing shard sparking with pink and orange lightning.

"Cool, it looks nice," Jeff said. The ministrosity gnawed on a bone happily. Observing this, Jeff gave him a bone and this tamed the ministrosity immediately. Jeff ran and the ministrosity followed him. "So, I don't need to put it in my bag," Jeff pondered.

Jeff kept running until an unexpected structure came up.

It was a massive fortress with breaking bridges, withered rascals, withered skeletons, husks, and the rocky imbecile. Jeff, like every lunatic, decided to climb up the fortress' bricks, trying to slip his fingers between the hot bricks cautiously.

Finally, he got on a wobbly wall and from there, onto a ruined bridge. He had a spectacular view of the dimension. He looked up to see an endless screen of stars and the mostly grey sky. A withered rascal focused on Jeff and brought out a metal claymore. The rascal ran around Jeff quickly and hit his back but Jeff was able to grab the rascal. He sadly swiped it with his glaive.

Jeff pondered on what to do, so he checked the box the rascal was holding. In it was a full set of iron armour. Jeff tried it on and conveniently, it was his size. The armour had the colour of a grey night sky. He then scanned through chests and was able to get his hands on a brick-shaped object. It had a weird symbol on it. Jeff threw the object up to the sky and it cracked upon crashing on the hard floor. An amethyst shard rose emerged from the shattered piece of brick. Jeff touched the shard and his appearance started to change. His eyes now glowing crystal purple, and his armour now purple. He also felt faster. "Woah! I feel different!" Jeff said with his voice now as vicious as a lion.

He dashed around the fortress, even running through the skeletons, until he got to a place where he saw the ancient holocausts. They were made of gold, with temperatures almost as hot as Venus. They were surrounded by golden bones which were on fire! Jeff didn't take chances; he looked at one holocaust's eyes and grinned.

He charged and slashed all of them multiple times; so fast that time seemed slow to him. Jeff was determined to destroy them, just like he did before. The flaming bones collapsed onto the floor and stopped burning. Jeff picked up a bone and his purple aura faded away, although his armour still had purple streaks on it. "Aargh! The power-up is gone! Oh well, I better get out of this place!" Jeff said. Suddenly, he saw a redminer approaching him. Jeff pierced the redminer in the chest and ran back to his portal. Immediately he arrived, he saw something coming his way.

Chapter 3

BAD BLITZ

Jeff got hit by a pig—a humanoid pig. The pig was static for a bit, and Jeff noticed its amazing armour; it had golden runes, a golden shoulder plate, a wooden chestplate and a golden helmet. The pig took out a golden axe and started whacking Jeff in the chest. "Ow! Stop it!" Jeff shouted. His ministrosity started gnawing on the pig's leg. The pig snorted. Jeff called it a "porker" because its snort sounded like the word. Jeff reached into his backpack and heard his kitty meowing happily. He grabbed the 11 gold ingots he kept. Jeff handed it to the porker, and the porker stopped attacking and gave him a pearl. Jeff handed him more, and the porker responded by giving him a black brick; it had a pig icon on it. Jeff smiled at the porker and ran back into his portal, but on his way, a rocky red dinosaur-looking figure emerged. It was horrifying. It looked like it could gobble Jeff up in seconds. Jeff had one option: to use jelly-bounce fungi—a mushroom that had an effect of bouncing anyone who jumped on it.

The real name for it in this dimension was jounce fungi. Jeff ran to the fungi and jumped on it and he was hurled through the air. He could see lots of things. His ministrosity was on his back, panicking. Jeff looked all around and saw something astonishing! It was a human. For the first time, he found another human in this dimension! The redminers were behind, getting shot into lava. Jeff was going for landing, aiming for the human. BOOM!! He landed in front of the human. He looked edgy. Jeff was astonished. He looked at the human's head and realised it was a bomb. Jeff tapped the head in confusion and it looked back at him. The bomb-head wore a teal hoodie and brown cargo pants; he had horrifying orange eyes.

"What do you want?" groaned the bomb-head. "Uuh hi, my name is Jeff. I saw you as I bounced on the fungi. What's your name?" Jeff stuttered. "I'm Whitty—Whitty Bomblitz," Whitty muttered. "Ok, uuuuh, so how old are you and, do you have kids-" Jeff asked.

"Don't talk about my kids or my wife!!" Whitty yelled.

"Why, it's just a question," Jeff said.

"It is more than a question! My wife left me for some ugly guy, and my only child died," Whitty cried. Jeff was surprised the man opened up that quickly.

"Oh, I'm sorry. Do you want to join us? We go on adventures?" Jeff asked.

"Ok, sure. But what do you mean us?" Whitty replied; Jeff didn't say anything. The redminers were coming, and an evoker spotted Jeff. It spoke an ancient language that summoned a set of teeth that almost snatched Jeff's legs. The evoker was coming hot, but when it spotted Whitty, it ran back to the redminers. Jeff looked at Whitty, amazed.

"Wow! Are you an outlaw?"

"Yes, I have broken the laws of Roland Maverick," Whitty said. They ran, dodging everything aimed at them.

Finally, they got to the portal. Jeff stepped through first, and then Whitty followed suit. They saw the decaying skull-fly, but it had an orange stone in its ribcage.

"We'll handle this another time," the boys said in sync as they got into the portal, but then they heard a voice.

"Hey!" said a woman named Carol, who had puffy black hair and brown skin. She wore a teal jumper and brown shorts and had muscular arms. She also had a pistol.

Carol was 24. She was the leader of a revered gang called the Exotics. The gang consisted of her and two others, Eddie and Gabby. Whitty started blushing as he looked into Carol's hazel eyes.

"I was wondering if you guys wanted to join the team," said Carol, with uncertainty.

"Yeah sure! We can join!" Jeff said, although a bit unsure. The decaying skull-fly started booming!

"RRROOOOOAAAAAAARRRRR!!!!!" the new decaying skull-fly roared and evolved.

"Let's get into the portal quickly," Carol insisted. Jeff stepped in first, but Whitty and Carol were wasting time, both insisting that the other go in first.

"Come on, you go, ladies first!" said Whitty.

"No, you can go first, I'm trying to fend off the skull-fly!" said Carol. Finally, Whitty stepped in, and Carol followed.

"Wow, she is...cool," Whitty thought. "Maybe I should tell her that-"

"Uhh, are you alright, Whitty? Honestly, I think you like Carol. You're falling for her," Jeff laughed.

"What have you heard or seen?" Whitty sneered.
"The fact that you were like, ladies first," Jeff teased further.

Whitty couldn't move. There was suddenly this blue aura around him. "Whitty?" said Jeff. "Yes?" said a wizard-like man. He was holding a book and a wand. "Who are you?" asked Jeff. "I am a mage of an ancient tribe...the cobalt celestials."

The mage wore a beige robe and had blue markings all over his body; he had a blue rune as well. He let go of Whitty and put down his book. "What are you doing?" asked Jeff as he watched the mage tap some sigils on his rune. "Oh, don't mind me," replied the mage. Jeff clasped his glaive. "Charge!" yelled Carol. She sprayed a rapid fire of bullets from her but the mage froze the bullets and sent them to the bomb-head, and BOOM!!

"AAAAAAAAAAAAAAAAAAAAAAAAAAAAAAAAAAAAAAA!!!" Jeff screamed as he got blasted into the depths of the wretched dimension. He had a hard landing and heard crucial meows from Joy. "Oh," Jeff moaned, "Where am I?"

Jeff got up, only to see a giant wretched wasteland. Lava flowed down and the only things present were black rocks and annoying species. The finger was a ghost-like monster that appeared and pointed at people. It pokes them with its sharp nails. Jeff frowned as his ministrosity stared at him.

"What are you looking at?" asked Jeff. The ministrosity's stare moved to a finger which was pointing at Jeff. "Welp, let's go." said Jeff. Immediately, a golem confronted them. "Huh? What are you?" asked Jeff.

The golem had a wooden tube mouth and wooden spear hands with mechanical arms. Its insides were hollow. The golem started shooting spears at Jeff from its tube mouth. "Uh oh..." Jeff said as he got hit by several spears. The ministrosity couldn't do anything. It was imbecilic. The golem stopped and smashed Jeff a few inches back. Finally, Jeff got an idea. He realised the golem was made of wood so he thought...wood burns when engulfed in fire, so the wooden golem would burn if soaked in molten lava.

Jeff grabbed the golem by its spear hand and brought it closer to the lava. The golem started shrieking so it hugged Jeff and inhaled his hoodie's horrible smell. Jeff reached into his backpack and brought out an invention he made back home. The yap. It was a ball that looked like it had teeth; it had to be thrown at the animal or monster he is trying to catch when it is worn out, and the ball will suck it in.

Jeff quickly linked the yap to his mechanical wristband and threw it at the golem, and the chassis got absorbed into the yap.

"I'm going to name it the wooden golem!" Jeff thought. Jeff trekked through the wastes, seeing things he shouldn't, like the scorched hand.

Jeff saw a geode, a boney and a tuff geode.

He made his way into the geode and saw something mysterious. It was a gauntlet, on the wardrock floor. Jeff was curious, so he touched it, and it summoned a hand.

"Ok, that wasn't a good idea. Fight, flight or freeze?" Jeff asked himself. The hand wore a black and red gauntlet and had an eye in its palm. Its pupil glowed red and it turned into a fist and charged at Jeff. It wounded him while he was still deciding whether to fight, flight or freeze. Jeff brought out his wooden golem, and it started shooting spears at the hand. The eye of the hand got fatally damaged. The wooden golem was pumped up, but suddenly another golem broke through the geode.

It was made out of rocks and had legs but no arms. It had a red sigil on its chest; the sigil was an image of a boulder. Its jaw was tremendous. The lower jaw was as big as a small TV, and the golem had three slit eyes. Its chest was a furnace and its legs were metamorphic rocks. The golem had one blue horn on its head. It shrieked. The hand blasted orange rays out of its fingers at Jeff. Jeff brought out his glaive and tried to slash the rays away, but it didn't work. He was wounded again, so he had one thing to do.

Jeff brought out an icy ring and placed it on the ground. The hand looked frightened. Jeff didn't care. A portal opened from within the ring and a hand stretched out—a hand with stubby clawed fingers. The hand had a mint colour with moss. Then the full thing climbed through the portal. It looked like a turtle, but with arms being dragged on the floor as the creature humped. The animal had a giant mouth with sharp razor teeth. It had small eyes and legs, and a volcano-looking shell. "I call this the gobbler!" said Jeff as the creature shrieked.

The hand cackled, "Ha! A turtle? How is that supposed to stop me?" The creature opened its gaping mouth to reveal 300 teeth.

The gobbler dug into the ground and spun the hand continuously! The creature then grabbed one of the hand's fingers, and it started roaring. "Just where I need it to be," said Jeff. The gobbler scratched the hand's eye, and Jeff aimed the wooden golem's tube at the eyeball, and... shots fired!

The hand started screaming while losing consciousness. Finally, it fell on the floor, dead. The gobbler got off the hand.

"Welp, now that that's done-" the gobbler was saying but got cut off by Jeff.

"You can speak?!"

"As a forgotten monster, yes, I can talk the same way fingers can." replied the gobbler.

"Cool!" Jeff said.

Jeff and the gobbler somehow became friends. When Jeff traversed the forgotten land, he made friends with the gobbler, and when he left, the gobbler started learning English. The gobbler was determined, trying to learn as much detail as possible! Two years later, the gobbler knew standard English!

Jeff heard a scream as a member of the cobalt celestials broke through the geode.

"He's over here!" the member yelled. It was a magic caller "Quick! In the portal!" the gobbler said, as it jumped into the portal. Jeff put his golem in the yap and eyed the magic caller, then he jumped in the portal, and it closed.

"Great." muttered the magic caller. The magic caller returned, looking around to see if the royal redminers were close by. The celestials and redminers were great enemies.

Chapter 4

THE FORGOTTEN LANDS

Jeff scampered through the forgotten lands, with ego running inside him. The gobbler led in front of him. The grass was light blue, and the trees were dry and drenched with heat, even though it wasn't hot. "Is time different here?" Jeff asked the gobbler. The gobbler nodded affirmatively. Jeff saw a lot of weird, disgusting, grotesque creatures. The jlellsquid, the rancher, the groteconj, the blobbers and more. However, there was one that stood out—the Tuffergol. It was a tuff figure who wore a red robe and normally gave information about objects. Jeff spotted one. It was holding a horn. It was as shiny as a unicorn's "corn" and as strong as a rhino. The tuffergol then spotted Jeff and made a slow run for it. "Really? You're making it hard for yourself," sighed Jeff, as he started chasing after it.

The gobbler smacked its hand on its face, disappointed. Jeff grabbed the horn and blew it, and then a portal opened. It was another world in there, or at least seemed like one. What came out was shocking! It was an impact golem. It smashed out and roared. It tried hitting Jeff but all he could do was dodge. He didn't want to break the horn or get severely injured. Impact golems are very dangerous; a bite from one could have Jeff sent to the hospital with 12 broken bones. The gobbler smashed the impact golem with its shell, but the impact golem redirected it at Jeff.

"Oh shocks," Jeff sighed. He started glowing and his horn disappeared. Joy escaped his bag, worrying about her surroundings and running into the forbidden woods. The glow turned red and stopped, leaving a red aura around Jeff. Jeff punched a very thick tree, and it started wobbling; it looked like it would fall with one more punch. "Oh yeah!" said Jeff, "This is awesome." Jeff started charging towards the impact golem and punched its sigil.

The impact golem's strength started wearing away. It shrieked and weakened and dug its head into the ground vigorously. The ground started cracking so Jeff punched it. *Physics changed;* the cracks immediately stopped and a portal appeared. It led to another future dimension. Jeff saw iron, blending with polished diorite, and a chicken. The chicken dashed out, striking the impact golem to its doom. The impact golem fell on its back, weakened. "Wow, a chicken has done all this?" said Jeff amazed, while throwing the yap at the golem. "Close off the security portal, I have to inspect this guy," said the chicken. It was wearing a tech backpack. At the back of the backpack was a reactor. It had beautiful feathers and on one of its wings was a certain tech watch device. "Seems like he is...Jeff?" said the chicken. "Fitzgerald?!" Jeff gasped.

Fitzgerald was a chicken professor, often known as the smartest chicken in the multiverse. He used to be Jeff's pet until Jeff abandoned him. "You are here!" Jeff squealed. "Shut up, moron," Fitzgerald grunted. "Why the attitude?" Jeff asked. Fitzgerald sighed. "You abandoned me, and you're asking?" Fitzgerald yelled and sighed again.

"I was practically the best pet to have. I made breakfast and gave you showers. I did everything for you, and you still left me to search for some stupid redmining people. What did you want me to do with my terrible life? I joined the tech-corps and started architecture and programming. Now I'm unstoppable and the best super chicken ever!" Fitzgerald said.

Jeff had fallen asleep while Fitzgerald was talking. "Oops, sorry," said Jeff as he woke up. "So, you killed that impact golem? What are you even doing here?" Jeff asked. "I have to take DNA from all golems and mix it in order to make an ultimate protector," Fitzgerald said bravely. "Right. How are there even portals?" Jeff asked. "I don't know if you heard about this; it's called the reality shift. It is a system whereby a person breaks a rift (the dimension between worlds) and makes a portal to another dimension." "Hold up... so my gobbler made a portal by hacking physics? That is crazy!" exclaimed Jeff. Fitzgerald sighed "You never listen, do you?"

Jeff glanced at Fitzgerald as he flapped his wings. He spotted a peg-looking creature on his wing, and a hologram robot chicken appeared from the watch. "Reginald, where is the reality crystal of this reality?" asked Fitzgerald in a deep voice.

"Go forward 8235cm squared chunks and then go 259 feet underground. The shard can be found in an ancient cave," stated Reginald. Reginald was a red hologram on Fitzgerald's peg-like figure. "What even is that thing on your wing? It looks like a peg," said Jeff. "It is called a spigot. Now I have an important mission-" Fitzgerald was saying, but got cut off. "I need that shard. It has to get back to the world of legends. I can't be stuck here forever with limited food supply," insisted Jeff. "You're not even gonna touch it. I need to bring it to tech-quarters," argued Fitzgerald. Jeff was already on the back of the gobbler heading to the crystal. "Oh no you don't." Fitzgerald snarled.

Chapter 5

UNITED PORTALS

The gobbler was sprinting with Jeff on his back, but Fitzgerald, using a jetpack, was flying quickly and dashed ahead. "Dang it, multiplier time," grunted Jeff. He got out a sticker with an X on it and slapped it onto the gobbler's cheek. He did this five times, and the gobbler started running faster and faster.

"Welp, I guess I'm having the shard for myself," said Fitzgerald. The gobbler stood still. "Where is Jeff?" asked the gobbler. "You broke his physics," said Fitzgerald with a tiny smirk.

"WHOOOOOAAAAAAAAAAA!" Jeff screamed as he zipped through the wormhole. He heard his parents' voices. Jeff shed a tear, fell on the grass, and saw the decaying skull-fly breathing directly on his face with a purple third eye. Jeff jumped up, startling the skull-fly a bit. Jeff heard a meow; it sounded like Joy. She jumped out of a bush and licked Jeff's face, "I missed you so much. Who's a good girl?" Jeff said.

The sky turned grey, and Joy got scared. "Quit playing games," grunted the decaying skull-fly. Its orange stone was glowing, and the fluffy clouds turned pitch black. The skull-fly then started absorbing the rocks and, soon after, the nearby animals.

Jeff quickly grabbed a stone just as the skull-fly was about to absorb it. Jeff ground the rock on his glaive.

His glaive was scorching, and red flaming fire was on the blade. "Okay, this is a fiery forge, just have to-" Jeff got cut off. "Fiery forge you say? Look at this!" screamed Roland Maverick. He didn't have his crown on. Something was off and he looked different. "Why are you here and what happened... king?" asked Jeff sarcastically. "I'm here to end you. Everyone hates me now, because of you. A hazmat person experimented on me. I lost my true face, I have a blobfish on my head, my family can't even look at me, and my mind is infested with this blobfish.

Look at me, look at what you've done!" Roland yelled. "Welp, sorry, blobface, but I don't want to be killed by a bunch of...idiots," said Jeff, laughing. "You won't be laughing when I do this!" exclaimed Roland.

The blobface blasted water out of his blob-mouth at Jeff's glaive, and Jeff poked the glaive at the blobface and made a run for it. "I have to get to Carol, Whitty, Eddie and Gabby," thought Jeff, but then a goblin shark shot out of the ground with blobface on its back. Blobface threw a pufferfish at Jeff. "OW!!" Jeff yelled as he turned green from the poison. Jeff began feeling nauseous and fell to the ground, unconscious.

Jeff woke up in his house as if nothing happened. Joy was playing with strings; Whitty was on a chair, sipping coffee bust with a busted head; Carol was watching TV with Gabby; and Eddie and Fitzgerald were staring at Jeff. "You lost consciousness, so Whitty carried you here," Fitzgerald said. "You're welcome," Whitty said. "Wha-what's going on? How are Gabby and Eddie here?" questioned Jeff. "Carol brought us here," Gabby said with a tiny smile. "You're a new part of the exotics, right?" asked Eddie. "Yeah, and this fellow chicken, Fitzgerald!" replied Jeff. Fitzgerald grabbed Jeff and took him to the corner of the room, away from everyone. "Why did you say that? You know I have a good job at Tech-Corps; they give me 30 pounds per shift," whispered Fitzgerald. "Chill... I'll tell Carol to give you 50 pounds per shift. Now, are you in?" replied Jeff. "I'm in," Fitzgerald said with no hesitation.

Whitty stood up and asked, "Uuuuuuh, are there any grenades or bombs here?" "Nope, you need one for your bombhead, right?" replied Jeff. "Just use this barrel full of gunpowder or this bag of gunpowder."

"I'll stick to the barrel," Whitty said. He placed it on his busted head, and it looked as good as new. He just had to carve holes for his eyes gently. "Guys, let me show you what I caught!" Jeff said. He brought out the yap, tapped it twice, and called out his golems, "Wooden golem, impact golem!"

The wooden golem and impact golem stood right in front of Jeff with their backs facing towards him. Joy screamed, "AAAAAAAA!!!"

"Nice, we just need a piece of it from each golem-" Fitzgerald got cut off. "NO, you're not taking any pieces," Jeff said sternly.

Chapter 6

MEGA-FIRE

"Okay guys, I'm heading out!" yelled Jeff. No one replied except for Fitzgerald, saying okay. Jeff stepped out and saw a burnt tree. He got closer, but then a puff of smoke appeared. He couldn't see through the smoke; he could only see a figure.

Jeff saw a humanoid robot with a goblin shark horn, a giant mouth with a sharp set of teeth and saliva, and a red crest. It had a flamethrower heart reactor, a V-shaped glass thing to replace the eyes, gauntlet forearms, and most importantly, fire hands and magma feet. "Who are you?" asked Jeff, hesitantly. "The name's Mega-Fire; I'm about to burn the world of legends with my redminers," growled the figure. Mega-Fire brought out burnt versions of the redminers, and a red-hazmat shot a fireball at Jeff's hand and, BANG!

Jeff woke up and found himself faced with a reflection of himself; he was in fiery form. His hair was spiked, and he had a baggier hoodie, baggier pants, red magma, a fiery gauntlet and no pupils. Jeff saw Mega-Fire behind him. He jumped 180 degrees and frowned at Mega-Fire. "You ruined me," growled Jeff. Then, a pair of lion ears stuck out of Jeff's head. He sighed. Jeff pounced on Mega-Fire, blasting several fireballs at him. Mega-Fire got out of the fire blast. Jeff came in with a kick from his swiftness boots but Mega-fire dodged it. His dodge hit just in the right place to strike Jeff, but Jeff's eyes turned orange. Mega-Fire put out his hand and made a small explosion. "Wait! Stop it, I'll leave, but have this," panicked Mega-Fire. He tossed Jeff a shard that was orange and pulsing pink. Jeff sighed and let Mega-Fire and his red-miners go.

"Welp, we won't be seeing any 'Mega-Arson' for now!" Eddie forced a smile, but no one laughed. "That was pointless," Whitty said, holding up a blunt pencil. No one laughed. Jeff returned to normal, smiling, knowing there was more to come.

Well, we all know that Jeff has gone on a bizarre adventure, although he will always have more to come!

The blobface is near...the saga continues.

www.ingramcontent.com/pod-product-compliance
Lightning Source LLC
LaVergne TN
LVHW040926150826
845672LV00007B/2230

* 9 7 8 9 7 8 6 0 8 1 7 5 5 *